'TIS THE
Gingerbread
Season

MONIQUE BRASHER

Monique Brasher

AUTHOR'S NOTE

'Tis the Gingerbread Season is the second story in my Enchanted Hollow series. My first book, *Meet Me At Midnight,* is about Laila's step-sister—based on Cinderella.

The Enchanted Hollow series is basically a mash-up of love letters to fairy tales, *Once Upon a Time,* small towns like Stars Hollow (Gilmore Girls), with a dose of emotional healing.

I'm a firm believer that good always wins, love *does* conquer all, and that the -ber months are the BEST time of the year. :)

I hope you enjoy Laila and Holden's very short and sweet romance! Grab a fuzzy blanket, some cookies, and enjoy your trip to Enchanted Hollow—whether it's your first trip or your second!

CHAPTER 1

LAILA

I'm lost. Not physically, but in every other sense.

Ever since the way things imploded in October at Ella's last working wedding, I've struggled to find where I belong. Old habits die hard, I suppose, since I'm right back in Enchanted Hollow. It doesn't matter where I go, my heart wants to be here.

Which makes me want to avoid it.

"The Reindeer Games take place at Ever After Farms. Yes ma'am. They're part of the Christmas Festival. Ah, no it's family games? You're not racing actual reindeer."

Sam's brows draw together and he mouths *'sorry'* so dramatically I have to stifle a laugh. He continues to explain that he's sold out of accommodation packages, answering more absurd questions.

The Enchanted Hollow Bed-and Breakfast has transformed since I was here last: deep red and green pillows dot the cozy living area at the front of the building, facing stuffed bookshelves and a roaring fire in the historic fireplace. Pine and cinnamon permeate the space, since I'd be willing to bet that all the greenery decorating the space is fresh.

There's a click as he sets the phone back into the cradle, followed by a heavy sigh.

"I'm so sorry, Laila. With all the Christmas activities here in town and on the farm, we're full. For weeks." Sam rubs a hand across the back of his neck, staring at his computer screen.

My future brother-in-law is tall, his handsome face set in a grimace like it's a *problem* that his sweet little bed-and-breakfast has no room for me.

I'm thrilled for him, even if I'm struggling to show him that.

"I'm a little disappointed that I can't race real reindeer. What kind of place are you running here?"

"It's kind of a liability issue," he shrugs, a smile playing around his lips. "I can offer everything—but a room—that comes with the Holly Jolly Holiday Escape, though."

"Save all of that for your guests, Sam. I'm just fine."

"Unless," he says, holding up a finger, "you want to share a room with the Anderson twins? But fair warning, they snore in harmony."

"As appealing as that offer sounds, Sam, I think I'm going to have to pass."

I should have given this more thought.

But as I ping-ponged across the country, diving full time into my influencer career the last couple of months, it's only further driven home the fact that I'm alone. Especially when I land in sweet little places where people are deeply in love with each other.

Watching my step-sister fall in love changed my brain chemistry. Nothing has been the same for me since, despite the fact that I encouraged all of it. Our jobs at Gilded Vows didn't follow the love story as it played out. We were just cogs in a machine, executing the perfect wedding day.

But now that I've seen what it looks like, I can't *unsee* it.

I shake my head, clearing my thoughts like an Etch-A-Sketch, and refocus on my current situation. The interior of this place isn't the only thing that looks different. I can't put my finger on it, but Sam seems a little less… polished?

That's not it. Sam has facial hair. Ever since my cajoling with Ella about men and facial hair, it seems like that's all I see now. That weird effect where you're not looking for something and suddenly it's *everywhere*.

Sam rubs his beard and grins. "I grew it for 'no-shave November' and I kinda like it. Thought I'd give it a more permanent test drive."

"Saw me staring, huh?"

"It's a new look. I'm not offended."

"It's not a *bad* look," I shrug.

Facial hair is an instant upgrade, if you ask me. Just look at Steve Carell. That and the whole 'silver fox' look. But that doesn't apply here.

Here, it's another reminder that everyone is moving forward and I seem to be stuck. Maybe even moving backwards.

Every Jackson sibling is gorgeous, and one day, Ella is going to add to the bunch. I rub my chest at the sudden pang in my chest.

"What if I call Mom? I bet she'd find a place for you at the house." He's so sweet, staring at me earnestly.

He probably mistook my gesture for something else, when really, I'm equally thrilled and heartbroken for my step-sister. *My sister.*

"I couldn't impose, Sam."

I'm also not sure I can handle being around their enormous family right now. That would probably make this feeling worse. As actively as I'm working to avoid my genuine emotions, I should put on some running shoes.

"After Luke and Ella are married, you'll be family too," he insists. "Mom would love to have you there."

My scarf feels like it's choking me. I want to be here, but I'd really hoped Ella and Luke could've waited to get married. I knew better, but I still hoped. There's a lot waiting here in this town for me to unpack and I'd rather do literally *anything* else but face my feelings. And you know, a certain someone.

Every visit until the one this past fall has always flown under the radar. Ella doesn't know that I've been back here for quick weekend stays over the years, hunkered down in a little historical apartment with a dark-haired baker. If she finds out our whole history, she'll return the encouragement I doled out to her tenfold.

I shudder.

Holden and I will eventually have to talk about what happened when I was here last. It's a *small* town. I can't avoid him forever. That's what grown-ups do, right? At least that's what Ella keeps insisting.

She's tossing the advice I gave her *right back in my face*.

My phone rings, a cheery Christmas tune floating in the air.

"Just a second." I smile at Sam and walk into the cozy library area that overlooks downtown Enchanted Hollow.

"Are you here?" Ella's voice screeches through the phone speaker, and I cringe.

"Yes, I'm here. Will you calm down?"

"Did Sam have a room?"

I glance back over at Sam, hunched over the welcome desk, frantically flipping through pages.

"No such luck."

"Come stay here then!"

I walk along the bookshelves, stuffed to the brim with volumes of books. Some paperbacks, some hardbacks, some

4

brand new and others vintage. I'm a little sad I can't stay here, curled up in front of that fire. It feels like a safe space.

At least until a memory of Holden reading me *A Christmas Carol* flashes into my mind unbidden and I turn away from the shelves completely.

Ella living on Ever After Farms is fitting. She temporarily moved into the Jackson farmhouse when Luke's mom insisted upon it. There was an incident with some freak cold weather and a fountain—something about the Mayor—and everyone decided it was best she stay protected until she got through her celebrity wedding.

But then Luke proposed–a lovely mirror of her own parents' love story–and she stayed. They live on opposite sides of the enormous farmhouse, but it's another thing that I'm struggling with.

I *love* that Ella is happy; that she finally found her place. But I wasn't expecting how lonely I'd feel when she did. My twin Bridget has echoed the sentiment. We've both noticed the massive hole in our lives since Ella came home.

Home.

I'm not sure I know what that feels like anymore. I thought I did, but again, Ella's stay here opened my eyes to a lot I've been avoiding.

Like I said: I'm *lost.*

"I can't do that," I say, refocusing on the conversation. "You need your space."

Her laugh teases a smile out of me. "If you think I have space in a house with ten other people in it, you're crazy."

"Not all ten still live there," I say, glancing again at Sam.

The whole Jackson family is nosy, and I don't need a certain someone knowing I'm here. Not until I can get settled and wrap my head around the fact that I'm here at all.

Again.

Right on cue, the front door bursts open, a flurry of snow blowing in with the bundled up figure.

"This cold snap is crazy!" he says, hurriedly closing the door behind him.

"Ella, I have to go." Despite her protests, I press 'end' on the phone and let my arm drop to my side.

Sneaky matchmaking town.

Or maybe it's a sneaky matchmaking future brother-in-law.

Holden unwraps his scarf from around his face and stomps his snow boots on the mat just inside the door. He turns to me, a goofy smile appearing.

Did *all* the men in this town grow beards?

Butterflies erupt in my belly as I take in this new, rugged version of him. When I last saw him in the fall, his skin was smooth. So smooth.

A ragged breath escapes me when I remember how his face felt against mine.

I may act like he's not, but Holden is an addiction for me. One I've tried to quit on multiple occasions, like people do when they delete social media apps from their phones. He's a dopamine hit with every smile, every hug, every 'hello'.

One look at him says I'm in *big* trouble.

"Sam says you need a place to stay?"

I turn and glare at him. "Are you a fairy godmother, too?"

"Way to be cool, Holden. Talk to you soon, Laila, I've got laundry to fold," he says, darting out of the room.

"Coward!" I shout after him.

It's mentally exerting to prevent myself from stepping into Holden's arms, letting him welcome me back. But that's not my place anymore.

"Is this everything?" Holden asks, pointing to my bag.

"You're not helping me."

"Sam said he's full, but I know the perfect place for you to stay—"

"I'm not staying with you." I shake my head. Standing here is hard enough. Nothing sounds more tortuous than being in close quarters of any capacity with Holden.

"Miss me?" His smile brightens and I swear the lights of the bed-and-breakfast flicker.

"Sure. Like a burr in my sock," I retort.

His megawatt smile falters for only a second before he takes the handle of my bag and lifts it. I'm being unfair—I *know* I'm being unfair—but this helps keep him at a distance.

"Before you say no, it's a historic house. Updated, with lots of room. Perfect for a city girl like you." His eyes twinkle with mischief.

Fine. We're doing this, I guess.

"As opposed to a small town hermit?"

"Don't take your hangry attitude out on me." He unzips his coat enough to retrieve a cellophane package from inside his coat. When he hands it to me, there's a little gingerbread girl holding a cell phone inside it.

It's really cute. And it's a splash of cold water on my poor attitude.

"I'm not hangry," I grumble as I unwrap it.

It's a subtle peace offering, even though he's not the one who needs to be extending the olive branch. He told me how he felt, and I didn't react the way he wanted me to.

"I promised your sister I'd bring you by the farm before I take you to your rental," he says, re-wrapping his face before motioning for me to do the same.

"I miss when it didn't snow here," I grumble. "Think this will go away anytime soon?"

"Maybe after the wedding." He opens the door for me, and I flinch at the cold that whips through the door.

With everything I've seen, it should be easy to accept that

Mayor Gold has a bit of a temper. One that affects the weather. But that's just it. I've *seen* it. And it makes me uneasy that it's still going on.

"At least Ella gets her white wedding," I say, following him down the stairs to his waiting car.

In true Holden fashion, it's running with the heat on. My eyes snag on the brightly colored cup from Once Upon a Brew, as we climb in. Eagerly, I peel away unnecessary layers.

"It's a Gingerbread Wishes Latte," he says, clearing his throat.

This is my second favorite coffee from this town, and we both know why he didn't bring me the first.

"Thanks."

I totally deserve to have to smell the spicy scent of cinnamon, cloves, and ginger all the way out to the farm. At least I can caffeinate while I suffer.

Like he can hear my thoughts, he sucks air through his teeth.

"It's decaf."

Awesome. Quinn isn't happy with me either.

This is a great start to the trip.

CHAPTER 2

LAILA

*E*ver After Farms has its own magical feel.

As families bustle around the property, snowflakes drift lazily from the sky between lights strung between sections of pre-cut trees. Signs point toward the u-cut section, and other areas of the farm like the Storybook Cafe or the gift shop. The scent of warm chocolate floats on the air, almost like it's reaching long fingers in my direction.

I know exactly how good the Wicked Witch brew tastes, if they still have it. The seasons don't exactly align, but the spicy Mexican hot cocoa fits the bill on a wintry day.

Holden ducks into the Storybook to make sure they're still doing okay on desserts and gingerbread, since apparently later today there will be several activities that involve them. While I'm sure he baked more than enough, I also know how delicious his cookies are. There's a good chance he needs to restock.

I follow the signs for The Gingerbread Trail, chuckling at the names and vibrant labels. After people leave the Nutcracker Bakery—or the cafe—they can head to The Candy Cane cottage, an adorable little booth overflowing with candy. There's a pathway decorated with huge candy canes and peppermint swirls, filled with trivia questions about gingerbread and Hansel and Gretel and Christmas traditions. My fingers itch to pull out my phone. The aesthetic is so unique and magical I want to plaster it everywhere.

But then again, that would make it easier for my mother to find me, though I'm sure she knows *exactly* where I am. Thanks to how things unfolded, I doubt she'd chase me here. It's the one place I'm probably safe from her.

I've somehow made it to the edge of the Christmas tree field, where more signs offer directions and random gingerbread man cutouts hide between fits to find. I pause, inhaling the scent of fresh trees.

"You seem lost."

I spin around to find the definition of tall, dark and handsome standing a few away. Sebastian Gold's exact image could go in a reference book, with a quiet broodiness and dark hair. Dark eyes. Dark clothes. He doesn't look angry, just stoic. Not even dangerous. Mysterious.

Like a less grumpy version of Scrooge or a version of Bucky Barnes without the mechanical arm. Although, that seems a lot less intriguing.

"Just taking a breather in the trees.," I gesture around me. "You don't happen to be looking for Jacob Marley do you?"

He barks out a laugh, catching me off guard.

"Super soldier serum?" I try again.

"I forgot how clever you are."

"Classic me—I'm quite the clever girl." I can't help but picture the scene in Jurassic Park where the trainer knows he's being hunted, and I'm not crazy about the parallels.

He hums for a moment. "More so than you believe, it appears. So tell me, why are you out here by yourself? I imagine Ella is happy to see you again, with all the wedding planning underway."

It intrigues me a little that I don't remember Sebastian much from before. It's not like I was paying much attention to anyone outside my circle of friends. I didn't even really pay that much attention to Ella for a while, and we lived in the same house.

Water under the bridge, I remind myself.

But it's more than that. His family is prominent here, between his family owning the bank and his sister being the mayor of Enchanted Hollow. I *should* remember more about him.

Despite things I've learned recently about him, I don't think he poses a threat to me directly. If I remove my mother from the equation, I like to consider myself a good judge of character and I suspect he's more misunderstood than anything else. There's no internal alarm warning me away from him, and there are a lot of people here today.

I take a few steps forward and pause, waiting for him to join me. The words flow easily once he does.

"For the sake of being vague—there's been some family fallout."

"I imagine so." He chuckles, and I shoot him a glare.

"Then you can imagine that I don't exactly want to be around my mother, and she doesn't want to be around me. Home doesn't feel like *home* at the moment, so I've been sort of—"

"Looking for a place to land?" he finishes before I can.

I pause, turning my attention to him. There's an understanding in his eyes I didn't expect to find.

"Actually, yes."

He nods and snow crunches under our feet as we continue deeper into the rows of trees.

11

"The tricky part is that you're searching for breadcrumbs to lead you there. Maybe you shouldn't be."

I'm not really searching for breadcrumbs. There's no need to. Every time I left here, the breadcrumbs laid themselves. I don't have to look hard to find signs of Holden, especially during the holidays.

He's in a baking display in any town I visit, or any wedding we serve. He's there when I see Tim Curry in anything—especially Home Alone 2—because it reminds me of the way we squeezed Clue in every visit. The movie or the board game. The man loves to solve a good murder mystery. He's in every piece of flannel, every classic Christmas song, every sprig of greenery I come across.

"Then what do you suggest?" I huff out, realizing a beat too late that he's probably the *wrong* person to ask that question.

"Sometimes you need to get lost to find where you belong," he answers.

"I'm plenty lost." I chuckle. "Wouldn't it be nice if it were as cut and dry as you say?"

"What do you mean?" Sebastian asks.

"I just mean, I wish we could see where we need to go in bright neon lights. Wouldn't that be nice? Hey, this guy is the one. This friend won't ever hurt you. Yes, this is the perfect career path for you."

We come to a stop and I realize we've completely passed through that part of the tree field. A whimsical watchtower reaches into the sky, ivy climbing the wooden planks. Christmas lights brighten this entire area, following the angles of the roof and expertly woven into greenery on the stairs and the treehouse balcony. Warm light somehow emits from the windows at the top, lanterns scattered at the bottom along with various Christmas decorations like more stinking gingerbread men.

I don't need to lay the breadcrumbs because they follow me no matter where I go.

"That kind of shortcut removes a lot of life lessons," he says.

"Maybe. I don't know what I'm saying."

"I think you know a lot more than you realize, Laila. Enjoy your afternoon and stay warm."

As he heads back in the direction we came from, I allow myself a few minutes before I need to get back and meet up with Ella and her little family. We'll come back this direction with her future step-daughter Lucy, completing each station. I'm sure there will be snacks and amazing memories.

More memories made with Holden, when nothing has changed. He doesn't want to leave and I can't stay.

I turn to go, and a sign catches my eye: *Welcome to the wishing tree.*

I just made multiple wishes out loud in front of Sebastian Gold.

Awesome.

CHAPTER 3

HOLDEN

*L*aila is quiet for most of the drive to the Wanderlust Refuge rental. The snow is falling harder now, almost at an alarming rate. Since the house is nestled out in the country, there aren't many lights and my visibility isn't great. I slow down a bit, grateful that I drive a SUV with four-wheel drive.

"Where are the snow plows? Sand?" Her fingers grip the console between us.

"La, this isn't Colorado. We've seen more snow in the last couple of months than we've seen in years. You should see the meteorologists try to explain it."

She tries to laugh, but the sound comes out choked.

I hesitate for probably half a second before I peel her hand off the leather and thread my fingers through hers. All the things I said back in October are a moot point under these circumstances. At this rate, I won't be able to drive back home and there's no way I'm leaving her alone in that house.

So we need to be grown-ups and put all that aside for now.

I risk a brief glance in her direction, and chuckle at her puffed-out cheeks. Her painted lips are blowing out a raspberry as she stares out the windshield.

Laila is strong and capable, and keeps her emotions locked down tighter than Fort Knox. Sometimes I think getting to know her deepest layers are about on par with finding out who killed JFK.

I slow down again, fine with taking longer to get there if driving one-handed helps soothe her nerves. Her shoulders are no longer near her ears. I don't want to tell myself that touching her calms her as much as it does me.

Every visit with Laila sends me deeper into the woods of wanting more. I'm not sure I could pinpoint the moment I knew I couldn't settle for a single cookie anymore and wanted the whole entire pan. Burned edges and all.

It's been simmering beneath the surface for a long time. But when she breezed into my bakery and straight into the kitchen, greeting me with a kiss that could've set off the fire alarm, I knew I had to actually *tell* her that.

And in true Laila fashion, she tried to pretend she didn't hear me. Like this hasn't been on the table for six years now. When she decided to pursue her career, I wasn't angry. I just didn't understand why she didn't think she could have both.

I've never given her an ultimatum; there's never been a 'pick me or pick your job'.

I simply told her that I wanted her for more than holiday weekends in the quiet. I want the boisterous Laila that gets excited over a carryout coffee cup, or looks for every photo op she can find. I want the woman who gives away more than half the products she earns doing her social media business.

When she was here in the fall, she filmed content for shops and refused to take a penny. She never mentioned it, but in the town meeting following that wild week in October, it's all I heard about.

I brush my fingers over her knuckles, wishing I could kiss them and offer her reassurance that I really don't want to go anywhere. But it's a realization she needs to come to on her own. I was reminded that I can't always be the one putting everything out there all the time—I deserve the same from her.

Which may be true, but after two months of silence, I'm reconsidering all of it. Pieces of Laila are better than nothing at all.

"How far do you think?" she asks.

"Just up ahead."

As soon as I say the words, lights from the old Victorian come into view. I've gotta admit, it's a welcome sight after miles of darkness and heavy snow.

"It looks like it's straight off a Christmas card," she murmurs, straightening in her seat to get a better look.

The service my brothers use did plow earlier today, but fresh snow has already covered the driveway again.

She drops my hand and I hate the absence it leaves.

"Be careful getting out," I warn.

"Not my first rodeo." She extends a leg and wiggles a snow boot in the air. "I'll be fine."

"Eventually," I grumble as she climbs out of the car.

Her 'leap before she looks' personality tends to get her into trouble and I don't think she'd like sporting a cast or crutches for Ella's wedding.

By the time I get to the trunk, she's spinning in front of the house, tongue out, catching snowflakes. The drifts by the driveway are a few feet deep and I hope the Jackson's prepared their crops accordingly. It's not like snow in Central Texas is something we see often.

I probably should warn her that this particular property

is known for its charm. And I don't just mean the exquisite details of its historical architecture.

It has a tendency to shift to meet the needs of the people who stay here. Some guests get really weirded out by it, but most people who come to Enchanted Hollow are looking for that sort of thing. So it usually works out.

By the time she heads inside, I'm only a few steps behind her. The first thing I notice when I cross the doorway isn't just the welcoming heat, it's the scent of cinnamon and pine.

But I know that they don't leave anything here that smells, in case people have allergies. This is a glimpse of Laila, the house already adapting to her desires.

"Wow," she breathes as I set her bag down between us. "This is so....cozy."

It is. The furniture is more rustic than I'd expect from her, blankets draped over the backs of couches and chairs, and Christmas is everywhere.

I watch her, looking for any clue that she recognizes what's happening.

"Maybe the house knew you'd be the next guest."

"That's silly," she scoffs. "I didn't even know I'd be the next guest."

"Wanderlust Refuge... it changes. It matches what people need for their stay. I guess it thought you could use a little Christmas magic."

She turns her head.

"Maybe it's right."

CHAPTER 4

HOLDEN

$\mathcal{I}$ think something is interfering with the cabin's charm.

This rental should have a minimum of four bedrooms, and so far, I've found *one*. The bed is set up in the coziest room in the house, with a fireplace I know Laila will love, but since there's no way I can make it back to town tonight, it's a problem.

I can sleep on the couch, but it won't matter. Laila will hate this.

When I find her, she's in the living room. Christmas music fills the space at a low volume, oldies. I'm a little surprised, because she usually is listening to the updated versions by current music stars.

"There's a small thing." I hold my thumb and forefinger up, leaving minimal room between the two. "Super small."

Her eyes lift from the snow globe she's holding. "Out with it."

"Well, there's supposed to be several bedrooms. There's only one with a bed in it though."

"One?" Her eyes widen and she sets the piece down on the table with a thud. "In the *whole* house?"

"That's exactly what I mean."

"There's no way," she says, brushing past me.

A couple of minutes later, she's leaning over the railing of the stairs. By the way her lips are flattened in a line, it's obvious she realizes I wasn't joking.

"I told you, La."

"What are we supposed to do?"

"Obviously, you take the bed. The couch doesn't look bad," I reply, jerking a thumb over my shoulder. "I can take that."

It's overstuffed and looks way more comfortable than the one at my house. There's even a lounge piece where I can stretch out on one solid cushion. I've slept in worse places.

"You're *not* doing that. You took time out of your day to chauffeur me around. You found this place. You should get the bed."

"Let's get one thing straight: I didn't 'chauffeur' you anywhere," I say, sure to emphasize the word with finger quotes.

"Semantics," she snaps. "I don't need the bed."

I cross my arms over my chest. "Well, you're not sleeping on that couch."

"Why not? It's beneath me?"

"That's not it at all," I huff. "I'm well aware you'd sleep in a treehouse in this weather just to prove a point."

"Is there a treehouse?" she asks, her voice softening.

"It's the bed or the couch. I'm not taking the bed while you sleep out here, comfortable as that couch may look."

"And I'm not taking the bed, so you can do the same." She comes down a couple of steps.

"We can settle it with a snowball fight?"

Her eyebrow arches. "Why not a coin toss?"

It's probably too much in our current situation to tell her that I enjoy seeing her fired up.

"More lively." I grin and shove my hands in my pockets.

"Fine. You win. We'll share. But there will be a pillow wall." She comes the rest of the way down the stairs and stalks past me.

"Are you sure you didn't want to share a bed with me? Remember, the house just does what you'll be comfortable with!" I call as I follow her toward the bedroom.

There's a frustrated shout as a pillow sails out the door and narrowly misses me.

Maybe I should go make some hot cocoa or sleepy time tea.

***

I'm being assaulted by the most extensive collection of pillows I've ever seen.

Apparently, Laila *loves* pillows. Considering how much she loves to cuddle, I'm not overly surprised by this. What does surprise me is her insistence that we divide a perfectly good bed.

"For clarification purposes, what do you expect me to do with these?"

"Build a wall." She gestures with her finger from the top of the bed to the bottom. "You stay on your side, and I'll stay on mine."

I scoff. "You can't be serious. I think we can be ad—" the pillow that hits my face muffles the rest of the word.

"We can be adults. But this just feels safer," she insists.

I'd like to point out that adults can have conversations without attacking with pillows, but I think I've ruffled enough feathers tonight.

"La. What are these pillows going to protect you from?"

She tugs one sweater sleeve down, curling her hand inside. Then another.

"I just feel better with them there. Okay?"

Her mood has completely shifted, and her vulnerability is on full display. It's rare.

"I can sleep on the couch if you're that worried that I can't keep my hands to myself."

"Holden." She deflates. "I trust you. I just… maybe don't trust me. You asked for boundaries before, and I want to respect that."

I asked for a relationship. But if that translated to boundaries, I'm not sure how to convince her otherwise. She blows out a breath and grabs her bag from the floor, ducking into the bathroom en suite.

A few minutes later she emerges, hurrying across the room like she's freezing. I started a fire, so she shouldn't be.

"Christmas pajamas?" There's no hiding the surprise in my voice.

She glances down, her cheeks blooming into an adorable blush. "So?"

"It's just not what I expected."

"Maybe a brand sent them to me and I'm testing them to see how to promote them." She pulls down her side of the comforter, avoiding eye contact with me.

"Did they?" I prompt.

Her blonde locks are swept into a simple ponytail, her face scrubbed clean of makeup. It's not a side Laila allows many people to see, and I know this is a big deal for her. But this is all I've wanted. I want her to let me all the way in. I'm tired of getting her in pieces.

"Why is this such a big deal to you? They're just pajamas."

"Why is this such a big deal to *you*?" I counter. "All I said is that it's not what I expected."

Her eyes lift to me then, and there's no mistaking the vulnerability there. Twice in one night.

"They're matching," she whispers.

"What?"

Laila huffs out a giant sigh. "I said *they're matching*. They match Ella and Bridget. We have matching pajamas."

More puzzle pieces click into place.

She had plans for this trip, and she's stuck in a house she's unfamiliar with away from her family. Despite our roller coaster relationship, I sensed the difference when she came back in the fall.

Laila keeps her feelings locked up tighter than a clamshell, so this new insight is like finding a pearl. It's rare and beautiful and I want more.

I pat the pillow wall she's created between us, urging her to join me.

"I'm a little jealous right now."

"You're jealous of our matching sleepwear," she says, narrowing her eyes at me.

The mattress shifts under her weight as she climbs on, keeping her distance.

"Technically, we sort of match. You've got Christmas plaid, I've got buffalo plaid. Plaid is plaid."

A smile plays around her lips. "Plaid is *not* plaid, Holden."

"It's a pattern."

"Very separate, distinct patterns." She shimmies under the blankets and tugs them up.

"How long have you worn matching pajamas?"

When I press for intimate details with Laila, she usually gets this deer in headlights look. Her whole body stiffens and you can see the protective armor shift into place. But for once, the way she tenses is less obvious. I just know her tells, so I can still see it.

"Well. It's a tradition we started when her dad was still alive," she says softly. "Ella was so excited for sisters. He gave us packages the night of Thanksgiving—he couldn't even wait until the next morning. He wanted us to have as many nights as we could in them."

It's mesmerizing to watch her recount these memories. Now I feel like the deer, frozen in place, so I don't spook her instead.

"They had their own family traditions, but we tried to start our own. They didn't last very long, of course." The happiness on her face flickers, like a short in an electrical fuse. "Ella, Bridget and I all lived together in Colorado. When we found our place, we restarted old traditions, and this one stuck." She shrugs.

"What else did you do?"

"You don't want to hear this." She shakes her head.

"Yes, I do La."

She faces me, the girl I knew from high school peeking out from behind the woman I've never stopped loving. I can't imagine losing one father, let alone two. Laila has worked hard the entire time I've known her to keep me in her little compartment, where she thinks I'm safe. It doesn't matter if she will admit that's what she's doing—I pay attention.

Laila is terrified of the consequences of loving someone, and I want to double down and prove to her it's worth the risk. Now more than ever.

I just wish she'd let me.

CHAPTER 5

LAILA

I can't remember the last time I slept so soundly. The sheets are soft, the blankets thick and honestly, it's like being wrapped up in a safe, warm cocoon.

There's a heaviness that is comforting, like a weighted blanket. Like Holden when we'd fall asleep on the couch watching movie marathons and woke up tangled together.

My eyes fly open.

There's an arm sprawled across my waist, and absolutely no trace of the pillow wall I insisted on last night. It's a little awkward, but I can shimmy out from underneath him. As long as he stays asleep, there's no reason to ever bring this up again.

I try to edge away from him, wincing when I find that first strip of cold sheet outside of our combined warmth.

Holden's arm tightens around my waist, tugging me closer.

"Where's my wife sneaking off to?" His voice is still gravelly from sleep.

Wife? WIFE?

"I was going to make coffee," I croak out, my head spinning.

He nuzzles my neck, his beard scratching against my skin. "I set the timer last night. Snuggle with me a few more minutes before the madness."

I need a decoder. A cheat code. Anything to clue me in on what alternate universe I'm living in.

A dream. This is probably a dream, right? Maybe I drank too much sleepy time tea before bed.

Squeezing my eyes shut, I count to ten Mississpppily.

One Mississippi...two Mississippi...

But as soon as I open them again, it's clear that this is very real. Whatever this is. To be extra sure, I pinch the skin of my forearm, hissing when I feel the bite of my nails.

Definitely not a dream, then.

"I should check on Ella. Make sure that they're not snowed in at the farm," I mumble. As much as I love Holden's arms, something is seriously off here.

"Were you having weird dreams again? It hasn't snowed here in years."

"What are you talking about?" I demand. "It snowed last night."

I shove myself away from him, throwing the covers away from me. Anxious to prove him wrong, I scramble out of bed, the frosty air like a bucket of cold water on my senses. Either the fire we had last night died off completely, or...

My eyes snag on the fireplace, no evidence in sight that one crackled inside the night before. I'm not in the cozy flannel pajamas I went to bed in. Instead, I'm wearing a soft cotton set covered in snowmen.

I can't even take a moment to enjoy how cute they are because I just don't understand what's happening right now.

With a shaky breath, I splay my fingers in front of me, intending to check my nails. When I went to bed, they were a

25

glossy cherry red, with candy cane stripes on the fourth finger of each hand. Precisely the finger that sports a glinty emerald on my *left hand*. It's a respectable one and a half carats—maybe even two—and I can't imagine where Holden would've gotten the money for something like this. Or when he gave it to me. Or why there's a wedding band below the engagement ring and another stacked above.

Wife status, confirmed.

There's an odd mix of terror and elation battling in my chest.

For the first time, I soak in the details of this room in the soft morning light. The walls are cream-colored now, with exposed wood beams stretching across the ceiling above us. I frantically look around, absorbing the Christmas decorations everywhere. There's a massive Christmas tree by the picture windows, stuffed to the brim with ornaments. Garland sprawls across the top of the headboard.

There are photos on the walls—*so many photos*—in frames on the dresser and nightstands. A well-documented love story of two people that chose each other.

"La, are you feeling okay?"

My eyes fly to Holden, half-awake and on his elbow, his dark hair tousled with sleep. He squints at me through one eye as he rubs the other.

"I don't know," I manage. "Maybe I just didn't sleep well."

"You didn't move all night." He tilts his head, studying me. He's concerned and I think he's got every right to be.

I think I might be suffering a psychotic break.

"But we had a pillow wall." I sigh, pressing my lips together. "This doesn't make any sense."

He raises an eyebrow. "A pillow wall?"

"When we got here, the house only had one bed, so we didn't have a choice. But you *promised* to stay on your side."

I hiccup, anxiety bubbling up in my chest.

"Honey, come back to bed for a few minutes." He motions with his hand.

"No." I shake my head. This is someone else's life. It's a beautiful life, but I don't belong here.

He tosses back the covers and makes his way to me. Dimly, I notice his pajamas match mine, and the ache in my chest grows. This is just a byproduct of our conversation last night. My imagination is going absolutely wild.

"This feels like more than a rough night's sleep." He hooks a hand around the back of my neck, curling his fingers against my skin and some of the tension in my chest unfurls with the tenderness. "Tell me about it."

"You'll think I'm crazy," I whisper, avoiding eye contact.

My heart is cracked wide open right now. On full display in a magical house where I'm the star of the life I've always secretly wanted, and I'm powerless to stop it.

"I think something has you rattled enough that it feels real to you. That's not crazy," he says. "It's valid to you, so it's valid to me."

There's a litany of other questions I want answers to, but there's one that feels the most pressing. I'm aware of the image my job has given me, but I need answers about this ring on my finger. Of all the reasons that I never committed to a future with Holden, money was *never* one of them.

But did I tell him that?

"What is this?" I point at the stack of rings on my very important finger.

"I'm pretty sure you know what that is. You were there for all of it."

Except that I wasn't.

"Humor me, please?" I sigh.

"I suppose you're looking for more than the obvious answer here."

"Please."

27

He pulls me closer with a gentle press of the fingers at my neck so he can kiss my forehead. It's a casual but intimate thing, something I'm sure he often does for this version of me. At least based on the way it seems second nature to him.

"If you want to see our wedding video again, all you have to do is ask," he murmurs against my skin, his lips spreading into a smile.

I wonder how many times he's done something similar, and I didn't appreciate it.

"This feels so *real*," I whisper.

"Why wouldn't it be, La? We're very real."

"It's too perfect."

Like a candy-coated gingerbread house.

"Perfection is an illusion. You, of all people, know that. The chaos, the messiness, the choosing—that's real. And I will always choose you."

But I didn't choose you.

He wraps his arms around me, drawing me into his chest. I've only been awake for a few minutes and I'm losing this battle. This is why Holden is the hardest thing for me to stay away from: he grounds me. For all I know, I picked the blue pill and I'm blissfully and ignorantly living in a simulation of my deepest desires.

Even if that's true: Holden is still Holden. *He's* real and I can focus on that.

"Why don't you take a few minutes and come down when you're ready? I'll start breakfast, and we can watch the wedding video while we eat. The kids want to go get the tree and decorate it today."

Kids??

My stomach flips, and I stare at him. "They want to do what?"

"I'll see you in a few minutes. Want a fire, too?"

I nod wordlessly.

Once he leaves, I glance around the room one more time, desperate for a detail that this isn't real. Proof that I'm being lied to, messed with, anything.

My eyes snag on the tree again, my attention dialing in on a specific ornament. One Holden gave me after a weekend visit. I rush over, eager to say what other secrets this tree holds and gasp when I notice that *all* of my gingerbread ornaments, the one Holden gives me after every single visit, are here.

Some are different. And they've multiplied.

How long have we been together?

I gingerly touch one, then another, like my fingerprints can unlock a transfer of memories to me and replace the ones I know. They're perfectly intact, solid beneath my fingers.

Did we go skiing on vacation? Am I in a coma? Do I have amnesia?

No, I wouldn't remember Holden.

Or would I? *Is selective amnesia a thing?*

I press my fingers to my eyes, sucking in a breath.

"I don't understand how this is real." I whisper.

None of this matches the life I know, but it certainly matches the one I've always wanted. The one I've believed for so long that I didn't deserve.

Sometimes you have to get lost to find where you belong.

I swallow the lump in my throat.

I don't belong here. The woman in these photos hanging on the walls looks like me, but she's not. This ring doesn't belong to me, it belongs to her.

This whole life isn't mine.

And I never realized until this moment how much I wish it could be.

CHAPTER 6

LAILA

The house has shifted since last night. The room I fell asleep in last night was downstairs, but this morning it's upstairs.

I take my time exploring the rooms, soaking in the tiny details. So much of our story plays out on the walls of our home.

Wedding photos on Ever After Farms, where Luke and Ella's family seems to be very much *my* family by extension. I was always so jealous of her relationship with them growing up, it gives me an odd sense of relief to know that love bloomed there.

Maternity photos where Holden cradles the swell of my belly, the love for this unborn child so apparent it takes my breath away. Am I as oblivious to the way Holden looks at me as Ella was with Luke? These images suggest yes.

Birth photos lead to newborn canvases, and then to photos of our children. I run my finger over the canvases, absorbing the nuances of these two little humans. The little girl is my clone. There would be no mistaking she's mine.

The boy is Holden's. I haven't even met them and I already love them so much.

How could photos of a life that doesn't exist make such an impact?

When he told me he wanted an actual relationship, not one that only worked for holidays or weekends, I was floored. Not because he wanted it, but because he asked. He's only ever asked once before.

And when I chose my career—which look where that got me—he understood. Time passed, and here we are. Unsure how to navigate each other because you can't just turn off feelings for someone, and we want two different things.

Knowing that I've only given him a full relationship one weekend out of the year when *this* is what we could have had just about knocks the breath out of me. I've robbed him of this.

I walk down the stairs, envious of the wood details and the lit garland that wraps all the way down the handrail. Lush and beautiful. And fresh.

As soon as my feet touch the bottom step, two heads pop up from a table in the living room and screams of 'Mommy' ensue. It's chaotic and loud, but the anger inside me shifts from myself to my own mother.

I sink down and bury my face against their heads, tears stinging my cheeks as they fight over who can get the closest to me. Bridget and I moved into an apartment not long after we graduated, because we finally realized the role we played with Charlotte Mitchell. We were pawns. As these high-pitched voices vie for my attention, telling me about their morning so far, I have another realization. My mother robbed me of *this*.

There's not one instance I can think of where she cared more about any of us than her image. She framed things so that it looked like she was interested in what was best for her

31

daughters—Ella not included—but it really was about what benefitted her most.

The Laila in this universe healed from the fear she'd do the same with her kids.

"They love you so much," Holden chuckles, crouching down beside me.

"Well, the feeling is mutual," I sniffle.

Nevermind the fact that I don't even know their names or how to be a mom. Just knowing that the potential for this exists for me—if I allow it—is enough. That wound inside me soothes, like aloe vera on a burn.

"I brought you coffee." He extends the cup to me, and I could kiss him for this act alone. But instead, I let myself *really* look at him. He doesn't look that dissimilar from the Holden of yesterday, but there's a clear distinction in his eyes. This Holden is satisfied with his life. I've never recognized it because I didn't know what it looked like.

The kids scramble off and excited squeals and the tumble of blocks become the soundtrack to this scene.

"You really did choose me," I whisper.

He presses the coffee cup into my hands and folds himself into a seated position on the hardwood floor beside me.

"You chose me back, honey."

"But, I was awful to you." It's blunt, but it's true. I don't even need to see more of what this life has to offer to recognize that. It's something I've forced myself to sit with the last couple of months when I realized how true that was.

"You're not going to do this today, okay?" He reaches out and tucks a hair behind my ear. "We're not going to go down the road of me deserving better than you and you doing the whole Peeta deserved better speech."

"How did you even—" My mouth falls open. That's exactly what I was thinking.

"I know you. And while this is a hotly debated topic—

especially with you," he grins, "I'd like to think my opinion of the matter is pretty important. Yeah?"

I nod.

"Then hear me when I say this: focusing on how to survive doesn't make you a bad person, La. You thought you were protecting me by loving me with stipulations."

I've never actually said those words to Holden. But he's right.

"You're so wise."

"I'm just a man who loves his wife."

I wish I could record those words, so I could play them anytime I wanted to.

"Even with all the flaws and baggage?" A lone tear drops into my coffee.

He shifts so he can use a thumb to wipe away the tear. "I loved you before you knew which baggage to take to the dump, La. Why wouldn't I love you now?"

"You did?"

I know this. He told me that he loved me. But hearing it phrased this way, so plainly, there's more impact.

He frowns and tips his head. "You're so different today. Are you sure you're okay? We can make it a chill day—stay here and hang out at home—"

"No. I want to do whatever you have planned. Everything you have planned."

"You sure?"

"I've never been more sure of anything in my life," I reply.

"Then come on Mrs. Lockwood. Let's finish breakfast and go get our tree."

CHAPTER 7

LAILA

*E*ver After Farms doesn't look much different as we
pull into the entrance. Fall decorations were everywhere the last time I was here, but now garland and bright
red bows adorn the signage. The Christmas lights are on
since it's an overcast winter day, but they'll truly shine when
the sun dips below the horizon.

Holden follows the winding dirt road to the parking lot,
and I swing the door open as soon as he shifts into park.

I haven't spent near as much time here as Ella, but it's a
comfort to know that some things have stayed the same. The
smell of pine trees and fresh-wood blending with the bakery
goods from The Storybook Cafe wrap around me like a
warm blanket immediately.

"Daddy—gingerbread!" Henry shouts from his car seat.

"Coming little man, hold on tight." Holden chuckles.

I open the back passenger door, where Luna is waiting
for me. We haven't spent much time together yet, but I
quickly noted two things. Yes, she's an adorable little cookie
cutter image of me, but inside, she's Holden. She's quiet and
watchful. Kind. Henry was fussy at breakfast and, without

34

hesitation, she reached over and gave him another piece of bacon. Followed by a second pancake.

"You look pretty today, Mommy." She says, her round eyes intent on my face.

"Thank you. So do you," I say as I wait for her to unbuckle.

"You look different."

I freeze as she swings her legs over to jump out of the truck. "Do I? How?"

"Dunno." She shrugs. "Can I get hot chocolate? And one of Daddy's cookies?"

What might look different about me today versus any other day in her world?

Cautiously, I say, "We can ask him."

"You do look different," Ella says, and I spin around relieved to see her.

I'm just not prepared for her shift in reality as well. She's got a navy blue beanie tugged down on her head and a baby strapped to her chest, two kids of varying ages underfoot, with an older version of Lucy at her side.

"You haven't even spent five seconds with me yet." My breath puffs out and hangs between us.

She narrows her eyes as she absently rubs the baby's back. "It's a feeling. Did you sleep well?"

"Why is everyone asking me that today?" I mutter.

Holden appears at my side, his hand hooking around my waist like it's something we do every day. "Ready to get the perfect tree?"

As our children erupt into excited cheers, I glance over at him. He's wearing a soft smile and everything about this casual intimacy feels so natural. Even though it's *not*.

"Yep," I whisper.

"Go find your cousins!" Ella says with a sweep of her arm.

We follow the kids through rows of evergreens, Holdens fingers laced through mine. More casual intimacy that I want to absorb like a sponge. It's hard to believe that I was here just yesterday, avoiding exactly this. Ella is glowing, which makes sense since she's got exactly what she's always wanted.

A husband, a family, love. Belonging.

"How's Luke?" I ask, aiming for vagueness.

"Somewhere out there arguing with Dean about the barrel car train and the tractor. Something about dried kolache jelly on the seat."

My laugh is genuine as it escapes—*this* feels absolutely normal.

"You seem so happy," she says. "It's a good look for you."

Luna brings us to a standstill, crashing into my legs.

"Mom, did you see?" She's pointing at a booth nestled in the trees, but my view is slightly obscured.

"What is it?"

"Mistletoe!" The kids all chorus.

A couple of steps later, and my vision verifies that they're correct. Signs like 'Meet Me in the Mistletoe' and '25 cents' adorn the booth, with garland and ribbons decorated the poles.

Ella shoots me a wicked smile. "I think you two need some luck."

She wants me to kiss Holden? The way he keeps gazing at me already has me in puddy form. I might melt completely if we kiss.

"We have plenty of luck. Maybe you should find *your* husband!" I laugh.

Ella's brows draw together. "You're turning down a chance with mistletoe?"

I'd like to have some words with alternate timeline Laila.

"Aunt Laila, it's tradition," Lucy insists. "You have to!"

Holden elbows me. When I look at him, his eyes are glistening with mischief. "It *is* a tradition. Hard to argue with that."

Of course it would be.

"You really can't ignore tradition." Ella's smile widens. "And luck."

"I'll remember this," I mumble under my breath as Holden tugs me toward the booth.

Luke's sister Violet is manning the booth, and she seems positively elated we're here. She swipes her braid off her shoulder and darts around to greet us, mistletoe in hand.

"You know the rules," she says in a sing-song voice.

She does her best to hold the mistletoe above us, but even standing on her toes, it's a failure. It's the thought that counts, right?

"It's a good thing I don't *need* mistletoe as an excuse to kiss my wife," he murmurs.

"Then what are we doing here?"

He steps closer, tugging me to his chest. "Tradition, remember?"

"Strange tradition," I whisper, wrapping my arms around his neck.

It's an old song and dance that feels second nature. Muscle memory.

The world falls away as he leans in, his lips brushing mine in a kiss that's both tender and unhurried. Ever since he showed up at the bed-and-breakfast, I've been wondering how it would feel to kiss him with a beard and the way it scrapes against my skin is a delicious new layer I wasn't expecting.

His fingers press against the small of my back and my body automatically takes another step into him, like it knows that's where I belong. I run a hand through the hair that's uncovered by his beanie, the other grasping his collar.

I take it back. This isn't second nature.

This is what Holden has been telling me for years, only he's not using words.

We break apart to applause and my face heats. I completely forgot we weren't the only people here. The kids are making gagging noises or have completely lost interest, while Violet and Ella and both whistling.

"Feeling lucky yet?" he whispers, brushing a stray hair out of my eyes.

I don't know how to answer when my mind and heart are both struggling for purchase. There's no way I'm looking Ella in the eye after that, because in an alternate timeline or not, she's going to see right through me.

And there's no way I'm having that conversation right now.

"Would you look at that?" Violet says from beside us, and I glance up.

Lazy snowflakes drift down the sky, almost like they're in slow motion.

"I thought you said it hasn't snowed in years," I say.

When Holden doesn't respond, I tear my gaze away from the sight of snow and my breath catches in my throat. The expression on his face is soft and full of wonder, a mirror of how my insides feel.

"It hasn't, La. Not since the weekend we got engaged."

It feels like we've just hit a pivotal moment, and I'm not sure what to do with it. Real life Laila would generally run from this sort of thing. But here there's nowhere to go, and I don't think I want to.

I think I want to see what else might happen. Like I'm being rewarded for that decision, the snow falls a little bit heavier and the kids explode into cheers about snowmen and snow angels.

It seems like the best way to spend an afternoon.

CHAPTER 8

LAILA

*T*he snow is spotty–but beautiful. It doesn't make it any less *cold.*. The winter air is blowing from the north and I'm thankful the former Coloradan in me was wise enough to keep stock in foot warmers. And gloves and fuzzy hats.

Ella wanted to keep the kids so we could have a 'date' and while I want to spend every second I can with them, I'm not opposed to a little one-on-one time with my handsome baker husband.

I could get used to that word.

We sit on the bench on the edge of Mirror Lake, lacing up our skates. I suppose when Mayor Sabrina Gold isn't angry; she does kind things like freezing the lake for everyone to enjoy. The ice gleams under the soft glow of string lights, the last bits of color slipping from the sky. Families and couples glide across the massive ice rink, classic Christmas songs pumping out of speakers attached to poles.

Holden is the first to stand, offering me his hand. "Ready?"

"Do I have a choice?" I laugh, gripping his hand as I push

to my feet. It's been a while since I've skated and while it may be like riding a bike, I'm wobbly.

"You never get better at this," he chuckles. "Skating isn't your strong suit."

"Yet you're amazing at everything you do," I shoot back with a smile.

"Only because I've got you by my side."

I open my mouth to tell him it's the cheesiest line I've ever heard, then close it again. Cheesy or not, I enjoy hearing it.

He guides me onto the ice, steadying me with firm hands on my waist. I'm not sure how I'm supposed to focus on staying upright when all I can think about is how comforting it feels.

"Relax honey," he says softly. "Trust me."

"I always do."

And it's true. Trusting Holden has *never* been the problem.

His eyes meet mine and all the outside noise fades as something deeper settles between us. Then his beautiful face splits into a grin and he's skating backward, pulling me with him like he's done this before.

We spend a long time simply cruising around the lake. I'm not sure why I won't allow myself to relax like this with him in real life versus whatever this is, because it's wonderful. He tells me about how The Magic Crumb is doing and all I want to do is listen because he's doing all the things he wanted to do.

"I know we've both been so busy lately, but I really wanted to say thank you. The schedule we came up with for the bakery truck is working out great, La. Every time we show up, there's a line waiting."

I'm not sure how to get him to answer all the questions I

have, so I say the one thing that I know can't be misinterpreted.

"I'm *so* proud of you."

"I wouldn't be here without you," he says, grinning like the teen Holden I remember so well, and my heart knocks in my chest.

"It's your talent, Holden. People can taste the heart you put into your food. And you're so good with people—" I stop because I'm about to comment on his interactions with kids at the Gingerbread Trail and that was real for *me* only yesterday.

Is that part of our history? Something similar?

"So are you. Laila, you're the one who exploded our business. Why can't you take more credit for that?"

I did, what?

In my shock, I trip over a divot in the ice and Holden is fast, catching me before I hit the ice and spinning me into his arms like he planned this all along.

"I've got you," he murmurs.

How does it feel like we're in that honeymoon stage? Technically, that's all we've ever really had, but this Holden didn't experience that. There's heat in his gaze that matches his teenage years, and I've never felt more beautiful.

More *seen*.

But only because I haven't allowed it.

We're only a breath away from each other. I wouldn't mind revisiting the kiss from the tree farm, especially without Ella or our children present. He's so close…

"Get a room!" a teenager cheers as they skate by.

We both burst into laughter. Holden helps me right myself, and we skate to the edge of the lake.

"Hot cocoa?" he asks with a lifted eyebrow.

"Sounds perfect."

He flashes me another grin before he skates to the exit,

and heads into the crowd. I follow, much more slowly, and practically run over someone as I attempt to get off the ice.

"I'm so sorry—" I say, pushing myself away from this tall stranger.

"No harm, no foul."

The whole world pauses as I raise my eyes to look at Sebastian. I let him guide me off the ice, mostly because he's the person I expected to see.

"Did you do this?" I finally ask, lowering myself to the bench.

He shrugs. "Technically, it was all you."

It's obvious it's magic, but it's different to have it confirmed.

"So what is this?" I ask, gesturing to everything before me. This life that feels so real but doesn't belong to me.

"A glimpse of what could've been. Or could be. Depending on how you look at it. I'm sure you've put two and two together by now, but in this life, you and Holden have been together for a long time."

My mind snags on three words: *or could be.*

"This could still happen?" I swallow.

"Not by my hand. This life is completely yours and Holden's. It's taken a lot of work for both of you to get here. A lot of love."

"I'm not afraid of work," I say, glancing toward where Holden is buying us warm drinks.

"You've never been afraid of work. You're just afraid of this." He points to his heart. "It's a scary thing."

"It feels so real," I whisper.

"It's not permanent, Laila. Charles Dickens was onto something with his ghosts. His methods were a little old school, but I think a glimpse is just enough to prove the point to even the most lost people."

"How long do I have?"

"It varies. It all comes down to a decision. Free will can be such a bother sometimes." He sighs. "But once you discover whatever you're looking for…"

I press my lips together. "So I could have a future *like* this, or things stay like they are?"

"Yes." His dark eyes gleam in the Christmas lights. "But you won't forget. Be sure that you can live with that."

How could I, though? I'm just supposed to snap back to my real life and walk through life knowing all this could exist for me?

But that's just it. *This* is magical. It's not real.

This could all shift and disappear, and I could go home to find that Holden is tired of waiting for me. Maybe he doesn't see this kind of future for us, or maybe he never did. I wouldn't really let him talk about it.

I never wanted to get so caught up in a relationship that it defined me. My mother married twice before she moved us away and even after we moved to Colorado, I *knew* another man had to be involved. I'm still not clear on all of those details. It's irrelevant really, because I don't have anything to say to her right now.

My ploy for us to be together for one weekend a year started so I could find myself without Holden. I didn't want to depend on him. I didn't want to be defined by him.

I didn't want to be like my mother.

The bench shifts as Holden drops onto the bench next to me. "You okay, honey? You look like you've seen a ghost."

"You're not too far off," I mumble, taking the cup from him.

He observes me quietly, but thankfully he doesn't press. "One more lap before we get the kids from your sister?"

I nod, allowing him to pull me up. Skating with hot cocoa

sounds like potential for a disaster, but I'll let him pull me around slowly. I want to savor whatever is left of this glimpse for as long as I can.

CHAPTER 9

LAILA

*T*he only time I've ever seen a kitchen this messy, was that time in Holden's commercial kitchen when we got into a food fight.

Flour dusts almost every available surface available, and cookies, frosting and candy over run our kitchen table.

Henry is standing in his chair, enthusiastically squeezing frosting onto every available square inch of gingerbread he can see. Luna is bent over her gingerbread house, tongue between her teeth as she frames windows and doors.

"She's really serious about this," I say to Holden, popping a gumdrop into my mouth.

"Mommy steal!" Henry gasps, dropping his frosting and pointing a chubby finger at me. "Give me. My turn."

"It's the Mommy tax," I insist, grabbing yet another.

"Caught red-handed." Holden laughs.

"I want one!" Henry squeals excitedly. "Blue!"

"It's kind of late. Should I let him have one?" I keep expecting my non-motherhood experience is going to out me, but Holden just gives me occasional funny looks instead.

"I think after the day they've had, it will be fine."

"One," I caution, holding up a finger for extra emphasis.

Henry giggles and grabs three. I'm too blissfully happy and fulfilled to care.

"We've got a structural problem on house four." Holden makes an explosion sound as a whole side of his house falls. "I'm out of the running, I guess."

"Well, if someone would stop eating all the support beams..."

"Hearsay." He slaps a hand on the table with a wide smile.

"I don't think that word means what you think it means."

Luna lets out an exaggerated huff. "If you two are going to be silly, will you please go somewhere else? You're ruining my Christmas lights."

I've never heard such a well-spoken four-year-old in my life. I also don't think I've been admonished by a child before.

"Daddy is sorry—no more table slapping. Your lights are beautiful."

She pauses to flash him a smile, then goes back to her work. "Mommy keeps bumping the table, too."

I drop my mouth open and hold my hands up in mock surrender. "I will make sure to not touch the table. Right after, I see if I can fix this wall."

Holden leans close to me. "You bought the strawberry candy canes, Laila. You can't expect me to exercise self-control when you buy the *strawberry* ones."

I have one memory of strawberry candy canes, and I find it hard to believe that we're referencing the same thing.

"What's the big deal about strawberry candy canes?" I ask, feigning nonchalance.

He's made a mess of his gingerbread house, probably to lose to our children because Holden is the *king* of ginger-bread houses, and I have to really lean in to see if there's any saving his destruction.

There's no reason to be taking it this seriously, except that this is the most fun I've had in ages.

"You're joking, right?" he says.

I blindly reach for the nearest tube. "No."

Maybe I can squeeze a bunch of frosting between the candy cane in question—which isn't tall enough to offer support—and close the gap.

"You bought them for me the weekend we got engaged."

I jerk in surprise, squeezing the tube, which is aimed right at my face.

Holden's laughter rumbles through the room, soon to be joined by our children.

"Gingerbread man!" Henry squeals. "Gumdrop buttons."

"You said we couldn't put frosting on our face," Luna says with a small giggle. "You look silly, Mommy."

"That's why we check the frosting tube before we squeeze," I reply. "How bad is it, Holden?"

His face is red from holding in his laughter. "Hold still, okay?"

"Frozen like a statue."

"Let it gooooooo!" Henry howls.

"How am I supposed to work in this?" Luna says, dropping her frosting.

Holden and I both burst into laughter. Without thinking, I swipe frosting off my face and drag my finger down his cheek.

His eyes widen in surprise. "That, ma'am, was a declaration of war."

Holden grabs a glob of frosting, smearing it across the bridge of my nose before I can dodge out of his way. I gasp, a mix of indignation and amusement, and reach for the bowl of sprinkles.

"You wouldn't dare." His voice is low, equally a challenge

47

and a question. Laughter dances in his eyes as he shoves to his feet.

"I might." I challenge, cradling the bowl, one hand already full of sprinkles.

Suddenly everyone is out of their chairs and it's a full out war.

Luna and Henry shriek and giggle as we weave and circle between our poor table and the kitchen island. Holden darts one way and then the other to prevent me from getting me. I act like I'm lunging to the left and he goes to the left, but I'm quicker.

With a wicked laugh, I launch the sprinkles in the air, creating a short-lived sprinkle rainstorm in our kitchen.

"Alright. Laila." This time it's his hands up in a mock surrender. "You win."

I smirk and set the bowl on the table. "Triumph is mine!"

But right as I reach for a paper towel, I hear the unmistakable sound of graham crackers crunching in his hands.

"Don't you do it, Holden!" I squeal, covering my head as I turn to see him, grinning mischievously.

He takes one step toward me, then two. "Don't dish it out if you can't take it, honey."

"Please don't, I'm begging you!" I can hardly breathe from laughing so hard as he backs me into a corner.

The distance is closing between us and I'm trapped. Then a handful of graham crackers showers over my head and I close my eyes to avoid a painful crumb disaster.

"I can't believe you did that!" I exclaim, breathless and laughing.

He steps back, grinning. "Doesn't Mommy look beautiful?"

The kids cheer, and my heart hammers in my chest.

"That's going to take forever to get out of my hair."

He shrugs. "We have a tankless hot water heater. You've got as long as you need."

"In that case," I reply, lunging to grab the bowl of powdered sugar. Lightning quick, I toss a handful in his direction, coating him in a fine dusting of white.

The next few minutes descend into absolute chaos. I've got no clue how we'll get this place clean, and I'm sure we'll be finding sprinkles and gumdrops and crumbs for weeks. Different ingredients fly across the room as we all laugh until our sides hurt. Holden grabs me around the waist at one point, swinging me around to our screaming children's delight, and this is another moment I wish he could paint so I could carry it with me forever. I could just pull it out and look at it whenever I want to remember some of the best moments of my life.

When he sets me down, I lose my balance and pitch forward onto his chest. Food fights shouldn't be sexy, but who am I kidding? Holden has never looked as attractive as he does right now, standing in our family kitchen, with Henry singing random songs in the background, and absolutely covered in food.

"You've got a little something—" He swipes a thumb across my cheek, then pauses.

"So do you," I whisper.

The air feels so charged I'd be afraid to light a candle.

His eyes drop to my lips, hovering for a moment before he's gazing into my eyes.

"You're so beautiful, La. I'm the luckiest man in the world."

"This blue frosting really brings out my eyes." I bat my lashes playfully.

"You should wear it more often."

"The powdered sugar really does wonderful things for you, too."

It's something to know that this version of Holden has seen me for the better part of six years. I'm unsure of the timeline here. But he looks at me the same way he does when we haven't seen each other in a year.

"Stop talking, La," he grins as he leans closer.

Luna giggles uncontrollably as Holden kisses me, and I have to admit, the teenage version of me does too.

CHAPTER 10

LAILA

We take turns cleaning the kitchen and the kids.

Holden insists that the rest will wait for morning, and we all pile into the living room. This time, all four of us have matching pajamas. Our newly decorated tree twinkles softly in the corner, and I cover both Luna and Henry in warm fuzzy blankets in various shades of plaid.

Maybe plaid *is* plaid after all.

Holden holds up a stack of Christmas DVDs and grins. "We've got Elf, Home Alone, The Grinch, and The Muppet Christmas Carol."

"No Scrooge. Scary." Henry pulls his blanket up so only his eyes are showing and I open my arms so he can scramble into them.

"He can be," I agree, glancing up at Holden. "Michael Caine really committed to that role."

"On second thought, ghosts before bed might be a bad idea," he whispers loudly.

"I know Santa!" Henry shouts, grinning up at me.

"Do you?"

"He means Elf," Luna says. "I want that one, too."

I think we really missed an opportunity here by not naming her Hermione.

LeviOsa, not LeviosA.

"Outnumbered. But Home Alone after," he says, glancing at me. "Another tradition."

My heart flutters a little faster. "Deal."

We've already let the kids stay up entirely too late—at least by what I consider normal standards—but I assume he means *just* us. As soon as he's done loading the movie, he drops into the space between Luna and I. He stretches an arm across the back of the couch inviting me into that space and I snuggle Henry closer as I do.

By the end of the opening credits, there's soft snoring coming from my lap. Henry's heavier, his little body pressed against mine. Luna giggles at the antics on television and every once in a while, Holden leans in to whisper funny commentary in my ear.

About a half hour in, Luna slumps against Holden's side.

"I guess we wore them out," I whisper, absently stroking Henry's hair.

"All those fun old-fashioned family Christmas shenanigans," he winks. "I'll go put them in bed."

"I can help. We're evenly matched, it just makes sense."

He chuckles as he scoops up Luna, and I cradle Henry close as we take them to their rooms. As I lay him in his bed, I can't help but go through the events of today and catalogue them away in my mind.

Sebastian said I'd remember no matter what, and I want to.

The family breakfast, the commentary during our wedding video, the tree farm, the quick carriage ride Holden snuck in before we picked up the kids, and everything once we got home. The decorating, the food—all of it.

Holden meets me in the hall to silently take my hand and lead me back to the living room. I settle on the couch while he turns off the lamps and soon it's just the two of us in the soft glow of the Christmas lights.

"Think you can hang in for Home Alone?" he asks, waving the DVD around.

"What's Christmas without eating junk and watching rubbish?"

"Perfect answer," he says.

He starts the movie and disappears into the kitchen. Moments later, he appears with an armful of Christmas tins.

"What are those?"

"I'm going to pretend you didn't ask that." He pulls off a lid to expose my favorite of his concoctions—gingerdoodles.

"You didn't have to go all in with the rubbish like that!" I scoot forward and swipe two from the tin, shoving one in my mouth almost immediately.

We settle into the cushions, and he pulls a blanket over both of us.

I only make it to the part when Kevin wakes up alone, before I can't ignore an unfinished conversation from the lake.

I don't know how much longer I've got here, so I want to make it count.

"You said I don't take enough credit for blowing up our business." My finger traces the rim of my coffee cup, round and round, so I can avoid his gaze.

"You don't, Laila. You rarely do."

"It's just a bunch of photos and videos," I mumble. "I tell people to buy stuff."

He touches my arm. "That's not even close to what you do. Can you look at me, please."

With a raise of my chin, I swift to see him. In the soft light of the Christmas lights and the fire, it's a little harder to read his expression but I can see enough to know he's being earnest.

"Your gifts in the kitchen are what keep people coming back. It's not me. It's just a fact," I say, gesturing to the tins of cookies on the coffee table. "*You* are always underestimating what you're capable of, too."

"That's what makes us perfect for each other." He smiles. "But you gave humanity to the bakery, honey. They're not just videos. You showed the history of my family. The hard work it's taken to get here. The social media pages, the website to the online ordering and the gift boxes. You organized all the hype for the food truck, and found the perfect locations to test an audience, coordinating all the menus and the businesses."

I suck in a breath. Somehow we found a balance and achieved our dreams *together*.

"You said we planned that together."

"Some of it. But you got the ball rolling and steered the ship. I just let you boss me around."

This is exactly what I want. Ella has been almost insufferable for the last two months—mostly because of how miserable I've been—going on and on about how amazing it is to have someone who encourages her and understands her.

And like an idiot, it's been under my nose *literally* almost half my life.

I confined it to weekends instead of letting it blossom into this incredible life.

"I love you," I whisper.

He's got no idea I've never told him this before, but I don't care. I'll let him anyway. Because I do.

"I love you, too"

He reaches over and takes my hand under the blanket, his fingers warm and steady against mine.

I don't want to go to sleep tonight. What if this is it? One day doesn't seem like enough. But that's the point, I guess.

If you find what you're looking for, you can't be lost anymore.

"This is real," I whisper to myself.

Holden's warmth is making me groggy, and soon my blinks last whole sections of the movie. Eventually, sleep overtakes me and I can't fight anymore.

This time, I'm more than happy to be missing a pillow wall.

CHAPTER 11

LAILA

*W*hen I wake up, there's no evidence that Holden was here at all.

I'm back in my plaid pajamas and as much as I love my sisters, I want to toss them in the fireplace and hunt down the ones that matched my entire family. There's a profound sense of grief I wasn't expecting.

Not over pajamas. Over all of it.

The husband, the children, the family that belongs to *me*. I got to create the schedule, plan the traditions–I made all the magic I wanted. And even better, I had a partner to do it with.

And he's been right there, patiently waiting for me this entire time.

I throw back the covers, shoving my feet into the Ugg clogs beside my bed and racing down the hall.

"Holden? Are you here?"

Nothing but silence meets me.

Maybe I really am too late. Maybe he really meant what he said.

The house is back to its generic coziness it was when we arrived, and the ghosts of what existed here only yesterday causes my heart to ache. My breaths come heavier as I search each room, coming up empty.

And wouldn't you know it? All the bedrooms have beds now.

The scent of coffee registers, and I practically sob in relief. He's still here somewhere. I'm too eager to care about how I look, or register the temperature outside because I *need* to find Holden as much as I need to breathe.

I throw the back door open, fully prepared to break into a sprint and hunt the surrounding woods. But I don't have to. He's stepping onto the porch with an armful of firewood.

"You're here. You're real." My words hang in the air between us as warm puffs of breath.

"Of course I'm real—"

I launch myself at him, ignoring the jabs of freshly cut firewood that digs into my skin to press my lips to his. He lets out a groan and pulls back slightly.

"What—"

He cuts me off with a shake of his head, then steps back so he can set down his load. Then his lips are on mine again. He's gentle and my entire body is alive with my newfound realizations. I tangle my hands in his hair, tugging him closer to me and the kiss explodes into everything we've been keeping inside.

Every kiss with Holden rocks my world, but there's a new element to this one. There's no holding back, no tentative dance, no 'we've been married for years'. All of that is etched on my heart forever.

But this moment? I wish Holden could paint it on an ornament.

We're finally in the same place and with the firm grip of

his hands on me, like he can't hold me tight enough, I'm on cloud nine. Ella's foot-pop theory has nothing on the magic between us right now.

When you know you want to spend forever with someone, it's a life-changing experience. Ella tried to tell me, but I couldn't understand. Family doesn't *have* to be the one you're born into—they're people who show up and love you in all your messiness and with all your baggage.

Even Sebastian tried to tell me.

Society makes us feel like it's a bad thing to not have everything figured out. We live in a society where so much of what we experience takes place with a screen. We film it, document it, share it.

But what are we really doing? Deep down? We're looking for connections. We're hoping someone will see that video or that photo and it will resonate. You'll matter.

Watching Ella fall in love with Luke changed my brain chemistry. But you know what else did? Living my life through the lens of my cell phone. Allowing my audience reach and the deals I landed and the amount in my influencer funds to determine my worth.

It mattered to my mother. But those things aren't what make me. They're not what make me a valuable person, or determine my worth.

Holden has known all of that about me from the get go. He patiently waited for me to figure it out and even though it's taken me twelve years to do it, I don't want any more weekends. I want every minute of every day.

"What's going on with you?" he asks, resting his forehead against mine when we finally break apart. "Last night—"

"I was an idiot last night. And in October. And every weekend before that."

"You're brilliant, La."

My heart sings. I pull away from him enough to miss the

point of contact, but I want to look him in the eyes when I say this.

"That's not what I mean. Holden, I've seen what we can be."

"I have too," he says, gripping my elbow.

"That's not what I mean," I say. "I saw it. All of it. We lived here. We had two kids—Luna and Henry—and they were perfect. The house was brimming with memories and so much love."

There's a squeeze in my chest, reminding me of everything I left behind.

"What else?"

"Luna is quiet, but so bright. She loves to be read to." Emotion clogs my throat as I think of her chubby little fingers wrapped around mine. "I just know she'll have your talents when she gets older. You should've seen the paintings on the fridge. Born talent. And she loves gingerbread."

"What about Henry?" he asks softly.

"He's not afraid of anything."

"So like his mama, then?"

It's amazing how easily I'm getting choked up over words lately. First 'wife', then 'mama'. I hadn't let myself believe it was something I could have.

"He's got a dark mop of hair like yours. But he never stops moving. He asked Santa for a puppy this Christmas."

I know none of it was *real*, but I wish I could see his reaction when he gets one. Holden said he'd get one from Luke when the new dachshund litter was old enough. My insides feel like they could burst from the want.

"You're right, I didn't mean that." The corner of his mouth lifts in a lop-sided smile. "But I want all of that, too. That's all I've ever wanted with you. And if you want to still do what you're doing now—"

59

"No." I shake my head. "I want this. If I'm going to work, I want it to mean something."

"You know you already mean something around here, La. I know what you did when you were here last, and I wish I knew sooner."

My cheeks heat. "You do?"

I should've done it back then. When I *almost* made that choice, and chickened out. And changed my entire path with Holden.

"Better late than never," he says, stroking my cheek.

"Someone told me that maybe I needed to get lost to find where I belong."

"And did you?"

"I think I've always known Holden. I'm sorry it took me so long to figure it out."

"I'm a patient man, La. I knew you were worth the wait."

His words echo the same thing 'glimpse' Holden told me. I wish I'd believed that so much sooner. But I believe it now.

"I love you," I whisper. "I choose *us*."

"Welcome home, honey." He smiles before he presses his lips against mine again.

'La' for a weekend was never enough. Now I get to be 'honey' for a lifetime.

I wonder if Holden has anything against being proposed to... because I'm *not* patient. And we've got a lot of catching up to do.

If you loved Laila and Holden's story, be sure and grab their bonus scenes here: https://BookHip.com/QWZTFGH

. . .

If you'd like a free fairy tale (short story) to kick off my Enchanted Springs series, subscribe to my newsletter via the link below: https://BookHip.com/VJXSABV.

Keep reading for a special recipe featured in 'Tis the Gingerbread Season...

GINGERBREAD COOKIE BARS

*G*ingerbread Cookie Bars:
- 3/4 cup unsalted butter (room temp)
- 1 cup granulated sugar
- 1/2 cup dark brown sugar firmly packed
- ½ teaspoon pure vanilla extract
- ⅓ cup molasses
- 1 large egg (room temp)
- 2 cups all-purpose flour
- 2 teaspoons baking soda
- 3/4 tablespoon ground cinnamon
- ½ teaspoon ground ginger
- ¼ teaspoon ground nutmeg
- ¼ teaspoon ground cloves
- ½ teaspoon salt

Cream Cheese Frosting:
- 6 oz cream cheese (room temp)
- 2.5 c unsalted butter (room temp)
- 2.5 c powdered sugar

- 1 tsp vanilla extract
- *Optional:* holiday sprinkles for decoration

Position the oven rack in the middle and preheat the oven to 350 degrees Fahrenheit—grease a 9×13-inch pan with non-stick cooking spray and set aside.

Step 1: In a large mixing bowl, mix together: *all-purpose flour, baking soda, ground cinnamon, ground ginger, ground nutmeg, ground cloves, and salt.*

Step 2: In a *separate* large mixing bowl or the bowl of a stand mixer, combine: *butter, granulated sugar, dark brown sugar, vanilla extract, and molasses.* Beat until fluffy.

Step 3: add the egg to the wet (sugar) mixture until evenly combined.

Step 4: Add the dry ingredients to the wet mixtures in parts (thirds works well for me). Add a third, mix for about a min-to a minute and a half. Repeat until everything is incorporated.

Step 5: put the dough in the pan, spreading it evenly. Bake for 15 to 20 minutes, or until the bars have darkened in color and a toothpick inserted into the center comes out with a few moist crumbs.

step 6: Remove from the oven and allow to cool completely on a wire rack before frosting.

Cream Cheese Frosting:

step 1: in large mixing bowl add cream cheese and butter. beat until fluffy.

step 2: slowly add powdered sugar and vanilla extract to the cream cheese mixture. mix on low until more incorporated, then speed it up and mix until smooth

Once the bars are cool, spread the cream cheese frosting on the

bars, add toppings and enjoy!

If you enjoyed 'Tis the Gingerbread Season, jingle all the way through the festive season with ELEVEN more Christmas novelettes that are like little bites of sweet and swoony delight. These heartwarming and feel-good romances feature second chances, enemies turned lovers, fake dating adventures, and more, all wrapped up in the cozy merriment of the holidays. Plus, there's a cookie recipe in each book!

Find out more here: Christmas Kisses and Cookie Crumbs

If you liked your *brief* visit to Enchanted Hollow, be sure to read Meet Me At Midnight and get to know more about Laila and her step-sister Ella!

ABOUT THE AUTHOR

Monique writes sweet, no-spice, small town romances. While they might have a smidge of angst, you'll always find a happily ever after with swoony couples and character growth. When she's not writing, she can be found watching The Big Bang Theory or Friends (or a Marvel movie), on the water with her family, or reading a book. She lives in Texas with her husband of 18 years, four kids, two dogs (Thor and Loki), and a cat.

facebook.com/moniquewritesromance
instagram.com/moniquewritesromance
tiktok.com/@moniquebrasherbooks
pinterest.com/moniquewritesromance

ALSO BY MONIQUE BRASHER

Pine Cove Springs series:

Technical reading order is as follows

Love at the Sugar Plum Inn

Love at the Christmas Tree Farm

Love at the Flower Cafe

Love From Pine Cove Springs (free bonus scenes)

Sweetheart Springs series:

Eggnog in the Evergreens

Sugar Cookie Christmas

Enchanted Hollow Series

modern fairy tale retellings set in a magical Texas town

The Farm of Forgotten Magic (freebie short fairy tale)

Meet Me At Midnight (*Cinderella*)

Christmas Kisses and Cookies Crumbs

'Tis the Gingerbread Season (*Hansel and Gretel*) — Dec 15, 2024

Made in United States
North Haven, CT
17 December 2024